This Book Belongs to:

_____

_____

For my friends & family

www.bugbuilders.com
Text Copyright © Bob Razi 2011
Illustrations Copyright © Bob Razi 2011
Graphic Design: Cherissa Kline
Editor: Tracy Heisler
Bob Razi has asserted his rights to be identified as the Author and Illustrator
of this work under the Copyright Designs and Patents Act, 1988.

ISBN   978-0-615-54576-9

BUG BUILDERS
HOME RESCUE
By Bobak Razi

"Boom, CRACK, **Boom!**"

Rain and lightening raged,
as the strong winds blew.

The house would not survive,
this storm far from through.

What they thought would last
forever, was all gone in a flash.

Concrete, wood and memories,
the entire house was **trash.**

The light of early morning,
revealed the damage done.

Crouching in the rubble,
were tiny little ones.

Who would have imagined,
anyone could survive.

But there was Molly Mayfly,
and her kids all still **alive.**

Molly called up her insurance,
the situation growing dire.

She was told they could do nothing,
her policy had **expired!**

Overcome by shock and grief,
she broke down and cried.

"How will we rebuild our home,
where will we all reside?"

Molly's cries for help,
did not fall on deaf ears.

The thought of what she'd lost,
broke Bosco down to tears.

"Don't worry Mrs. Mayfly
I'll do all I can.

Dry your tears and wipe
your eyes, I'll bring my
team and a plan.""

Lightening Bug Larry

and friends woke up early,
starting at dawn's first light.

Picking up the trash,
cleaning up the site.

Friends came from all around,
no way to do this alone.

If they all worked hard together,
they could build the Mayfly home.

Ray T. Bug surveys the land,
Spidey edges and trowels.

The concrete is pumped by
Wormy and Dan, while Larry
removing form boards follows.

The backhoe digs the underground,
as the sewers provide sanitation.

Life is a lot like a house,

you need a good **foundation.**

Wormy checks the
pitch of the pipes,
as the plumbing is going in.

Larry installs risers and treads,
he measures the height again.

Walls are nailed together,
then lifted into place.

Bosco's eye for architecture,
makes good use of **space.**

Roll E. Polly pulls the wire, running from box to box.

Lightening Bug Larry is careful, that no one gets a shock!

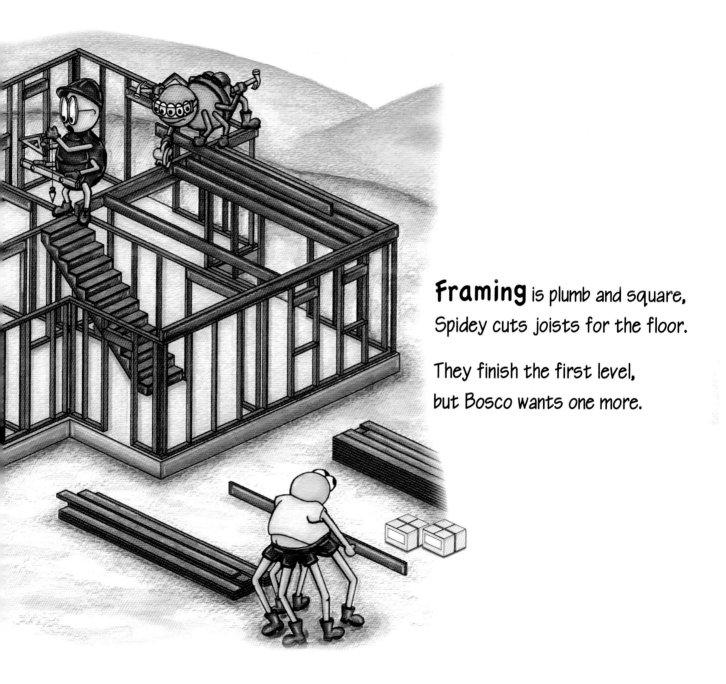

Framing is plumb and square,
Spidey cuts joists for the floor.

They finish the first level,
but Bosco wants one more.

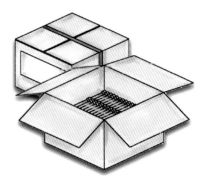

Spidey nails the subfloor,
as Wormy shores the wall.

The guys have to be careful,
Careful not to fall.

Second story is going up,
as Bosco checks the plans.

Ray T. Bug draws the layout,
as Bosco yells commands.

The guys mud and tape,
the framing almost completed.

Dan D. Longlegs
hangs the sheetrock,
while the studs are sheeted.

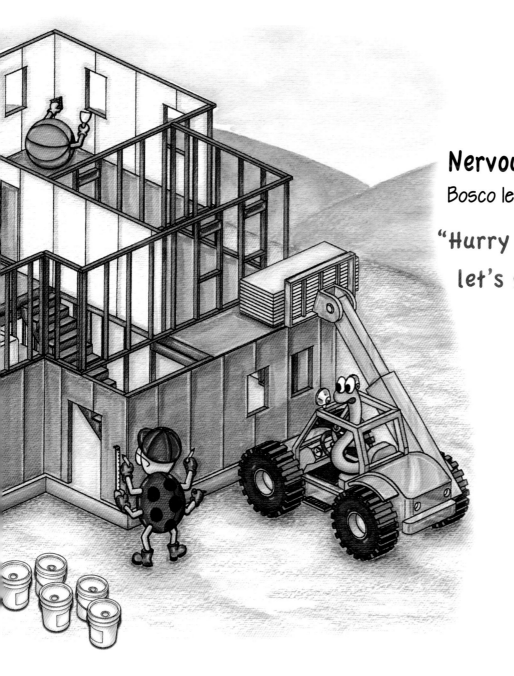

Nervous about the weather, Bosco lets them know.

"Hurry up, hurry up,
 let's go, go, **go!**"

Bosco guides the crane,
as Wormy finds the space.

Spidey is standing by,
nailing trusses into place.

Storms brewing overhead,
they need that roof soon.

If it started raining now,
all could end in ruin.

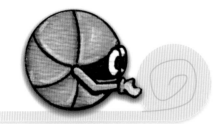

Lay down the roof felt,
to stop water penetration.

Nail down the shingles quick,
roll out the **insulation.**

Danger lurking in the sky,
the roof is almost done.

Storms took the last house,
but will not take this one.

Strong winds blew through the night, driving clouds away.

Installing windows and siding, it is going to be a nice day.

Bosco checks his **schedule,**
there are many things to do.

Hurry up with the landscape,
let's move in this Mayfly crew.

Wow! The family is speechless, as they gaze at their new home.

Overcome by tears of joy, and the love they all were shown.

Now it's time to go to sleep, as that's how this story ends.

Wouldn't life be great,

if we were all Bosco's **friends.**

Mrs. Molly Mayfly

Bosco

Spidey

Ray T. Bug